CUMBRIA LIBRARIES
3 8003 04850 1175
KT-407-998
This Orchard book
belongs to
....

TEN LITTLE ROBOTS

MIKE BROWNLOW ✿ SIMON RICKERTY

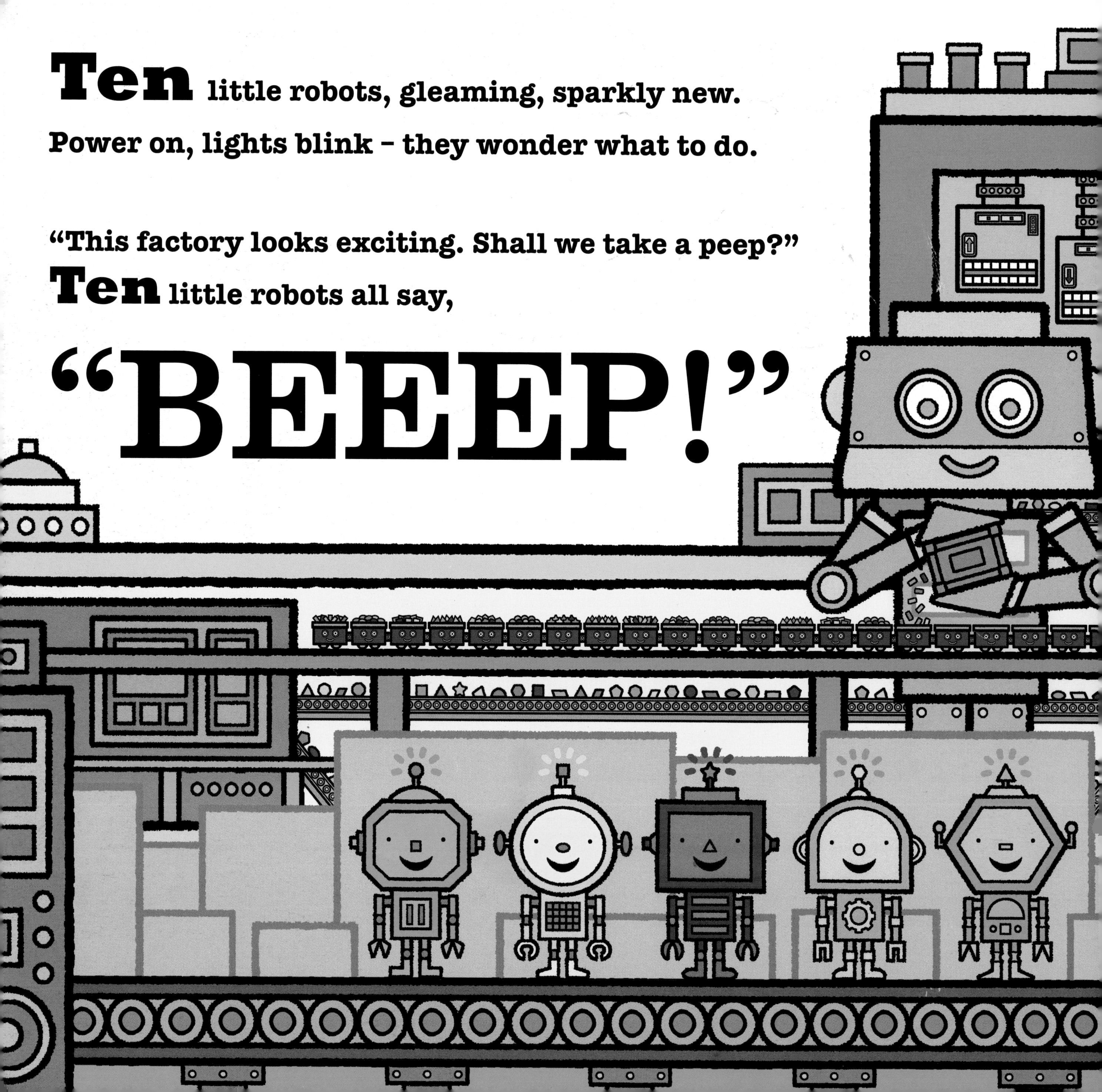

Ten little robots, gleaming, sparkly new.
Power on, lights blink – they wonder what to do.

"This factory looks exciting. Shall we take a peep?"
Ten little robots all say,

"BEEEP!"

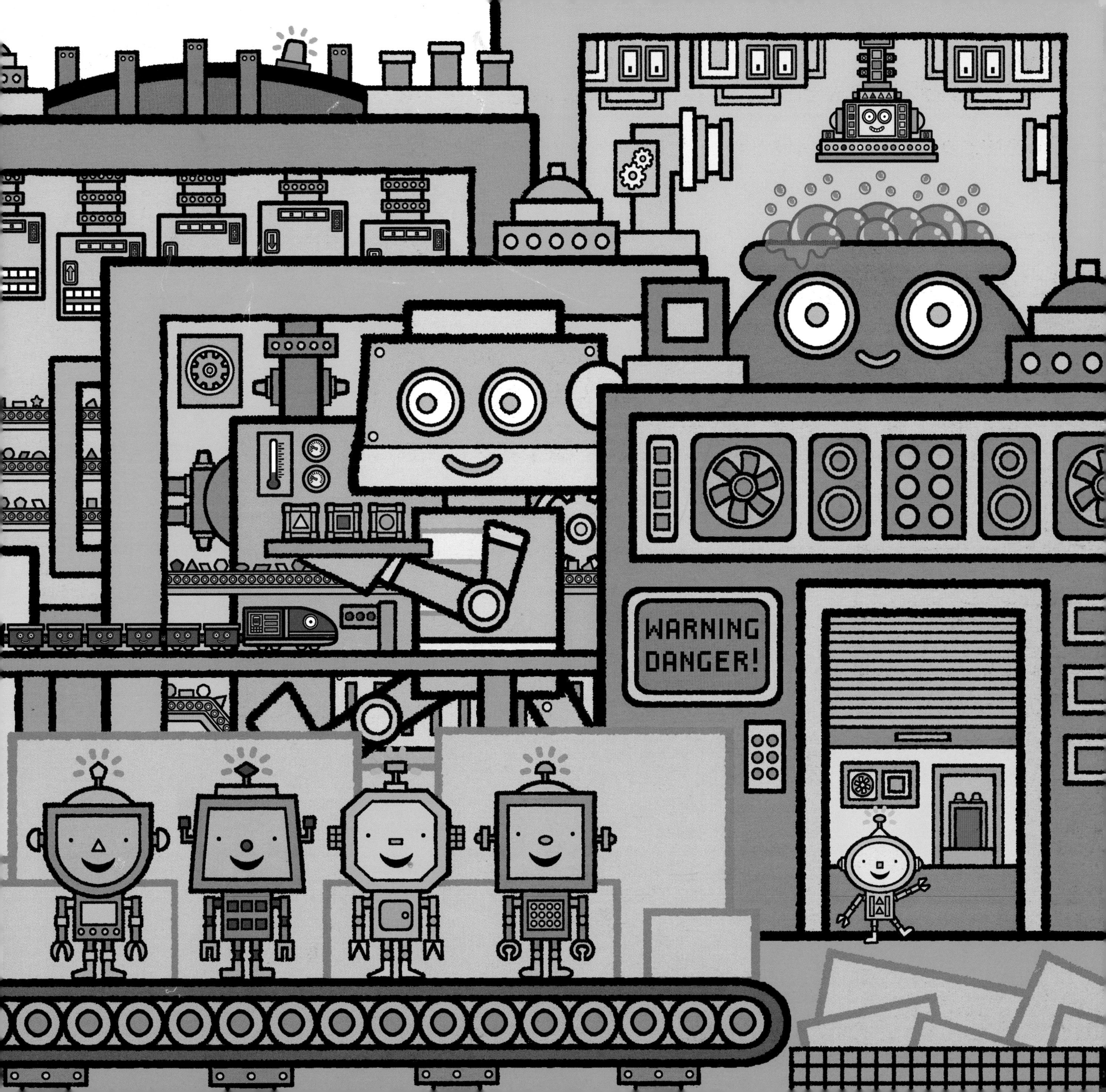
WARNING
DANGER!

Ten little robots miss a warning sign.
"NEEE NAA
10

AAH!"

goes the siren.

Now there are . . .

. . . nine.

Nine little robots

stumble through a gate.

"Whoops!"
Mind the slippy oil!
Now there are . . .

...eight.

Eight little robots – it’s hot just like an oven.

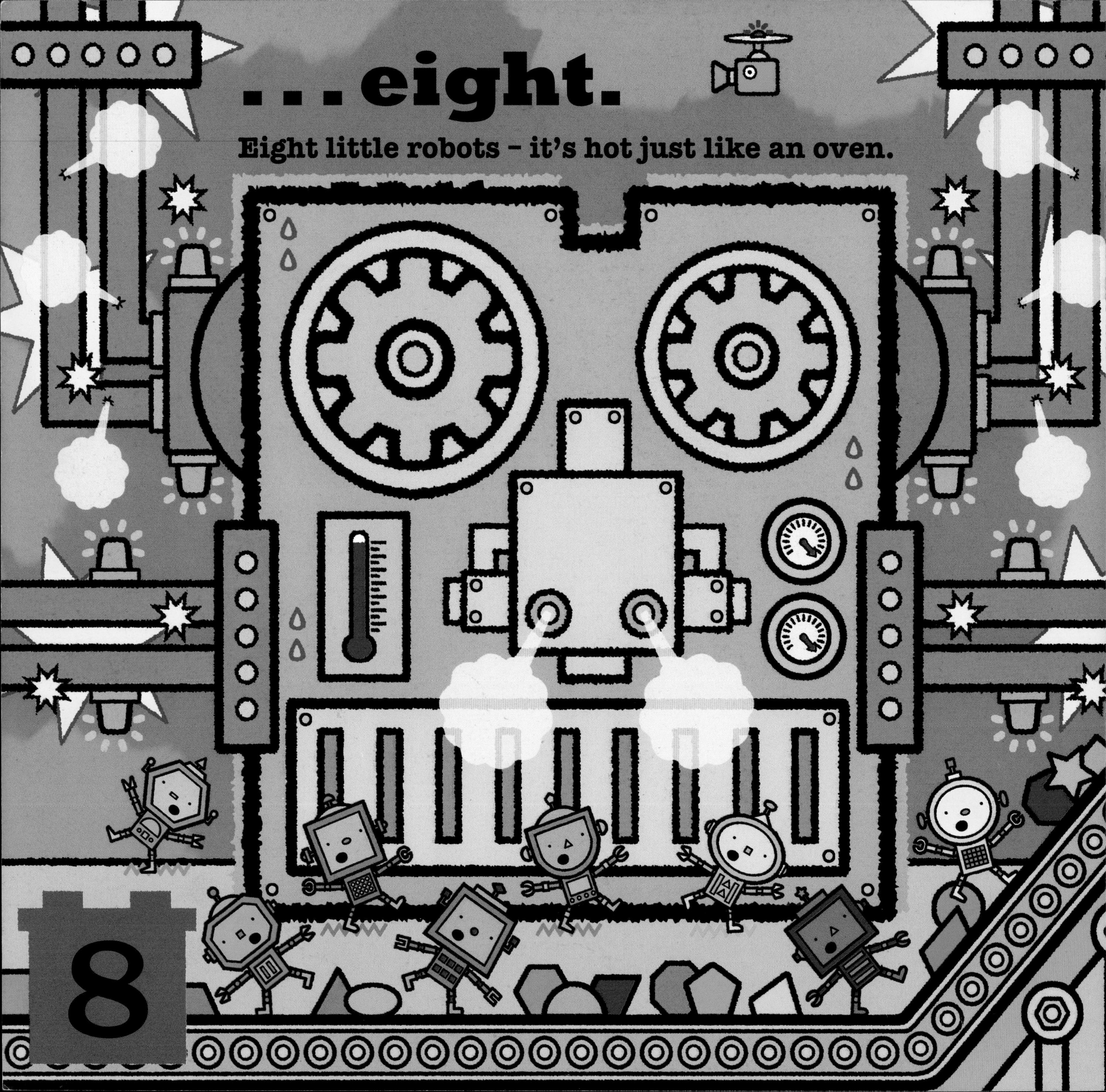

"KERBOOOOM!"
goes the engine room.
Now there are . . .

...seven.
Seven little robots
dodge the crashing bricks.
7
CHOOO CHO

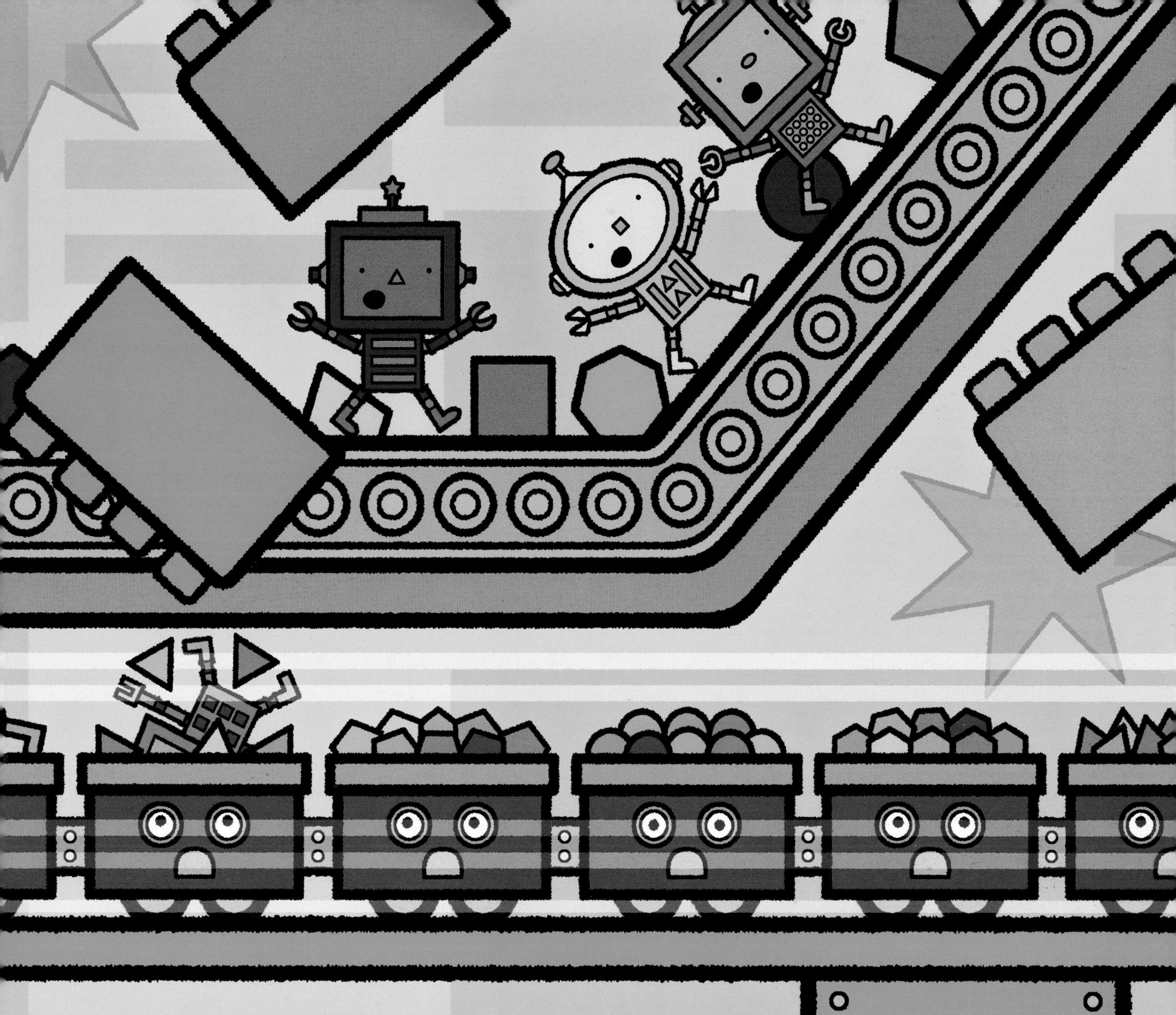

OO! goes the tiny train. Now there are . . .

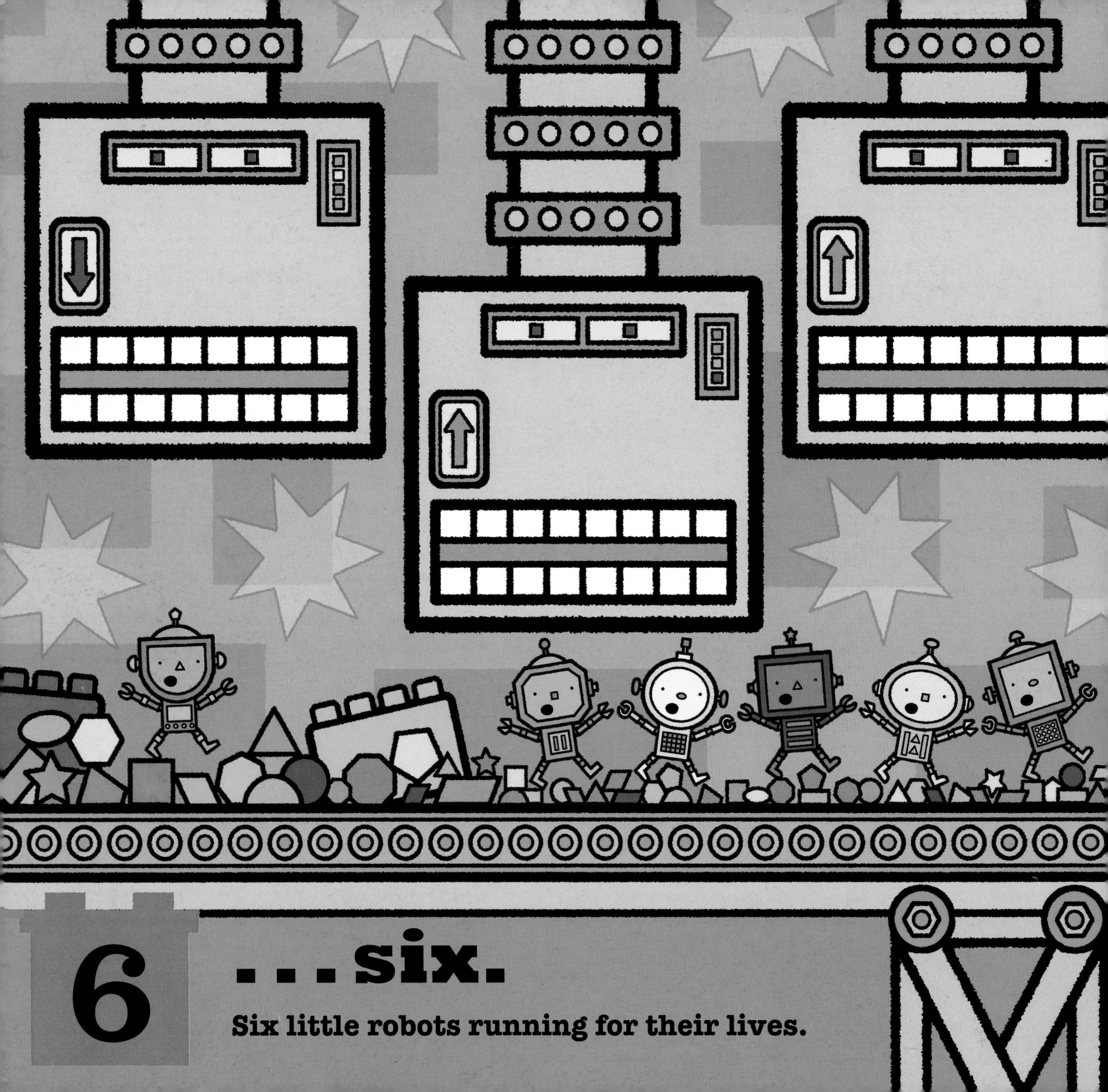
6
. . . six.
Six little robots running for their lives.

THUMP!
go the
crusher's
hammers.
Now there are . . .

. . . five.

Five little robots fear the furnace roar.

CLANG!
goes the magno-grab.
Now there
are . . .

. . . four.

Four little robots

trying to wriggle free.

BOING!
goes a flying spring.
Now there are . . .

. . . three.

Three little robots

above the

molten brew.

3

CRACKLE! FIZZLE!
go the sparks.
Now there are . . .

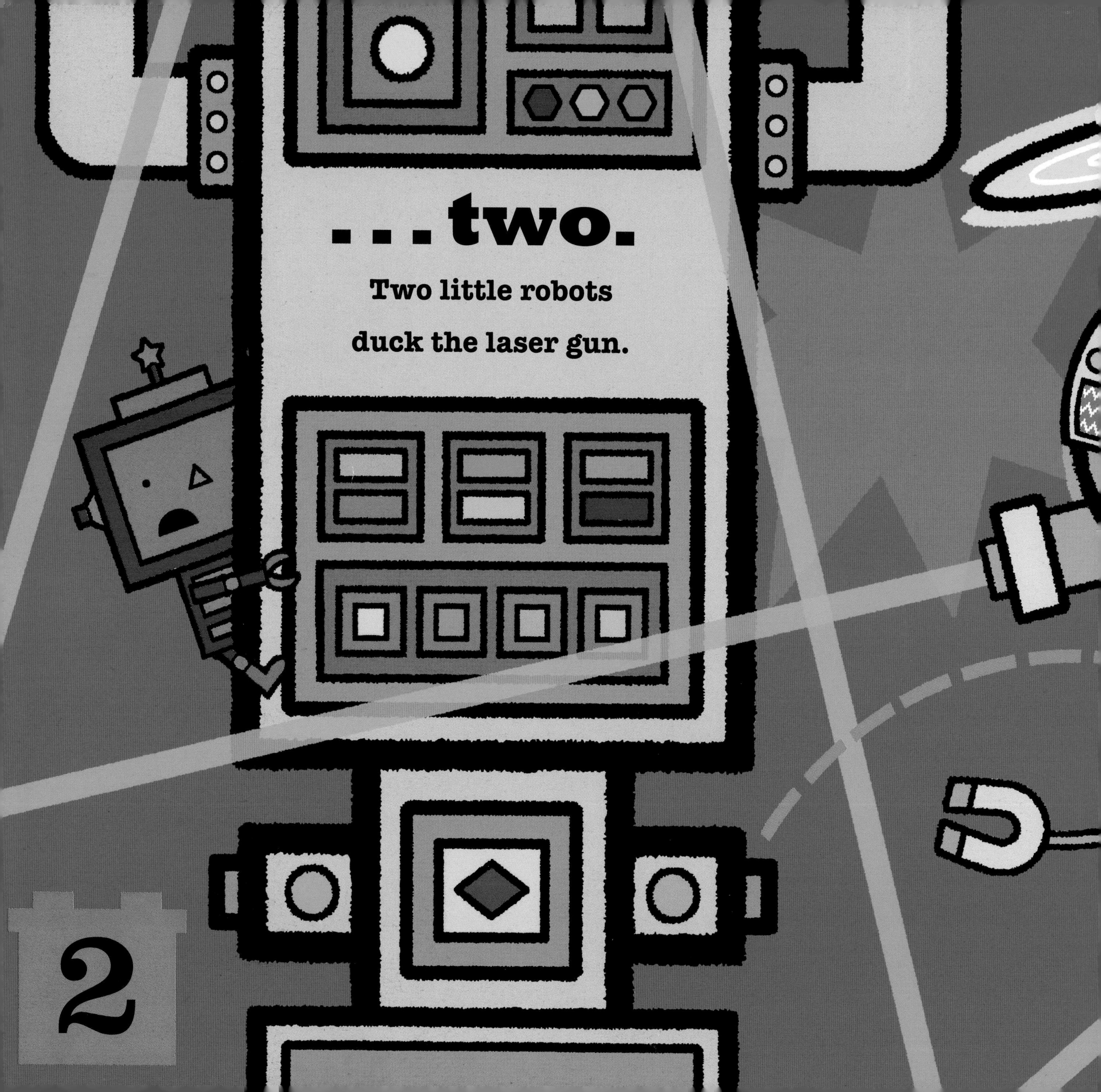
. . . two.
Two little robots
duck the laser gun.
2

BUZZZ!

whines the heli-drone.

Now there's only . . .

. . . one.
1

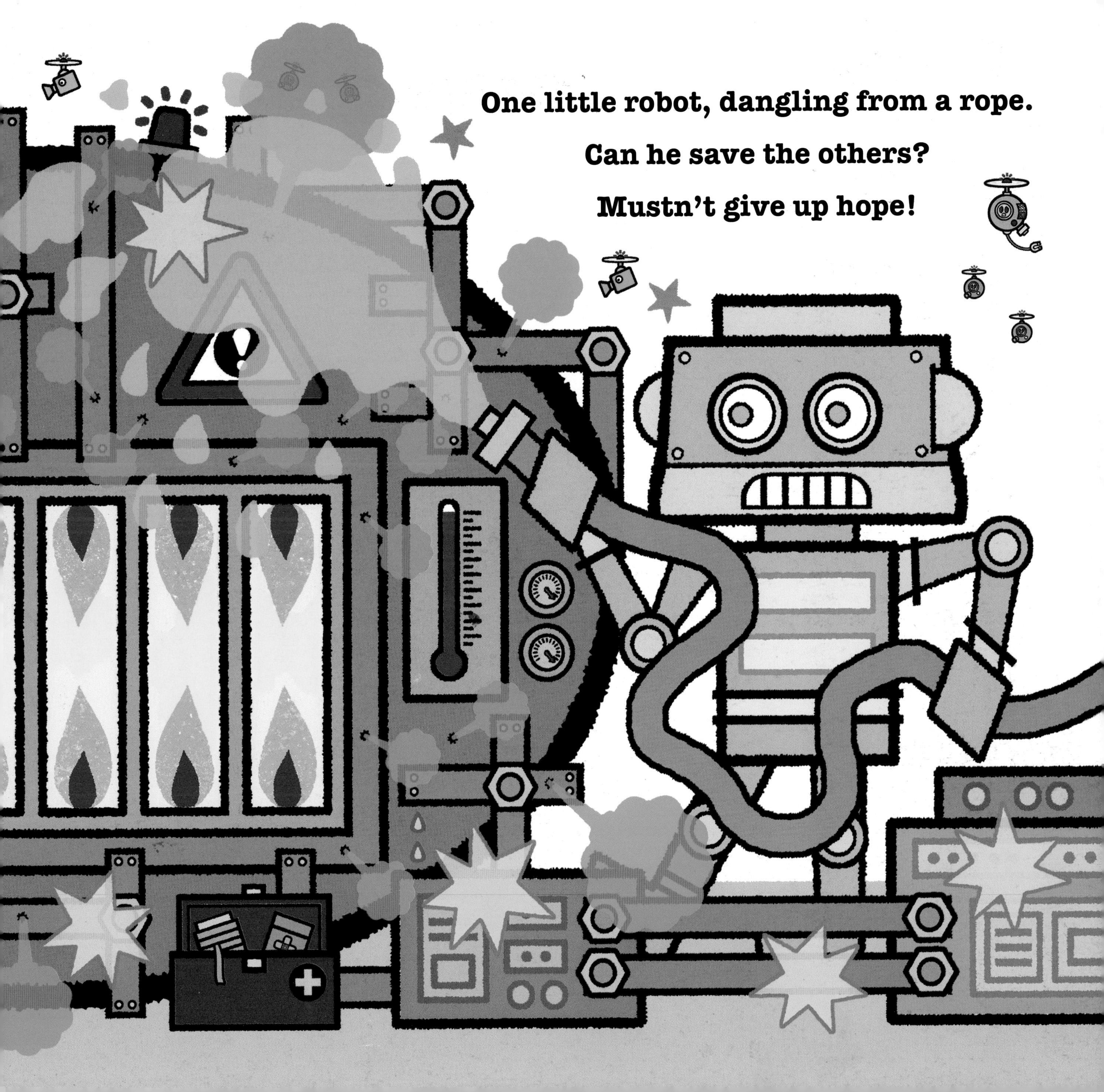

One little robot, dangling from a rope.

Can he save the others?

Mustn't give up hope!

Fighting through the wreckage,
climbing through the mess.
Plug the holes.

Fix the pipes.

Can he mend it?

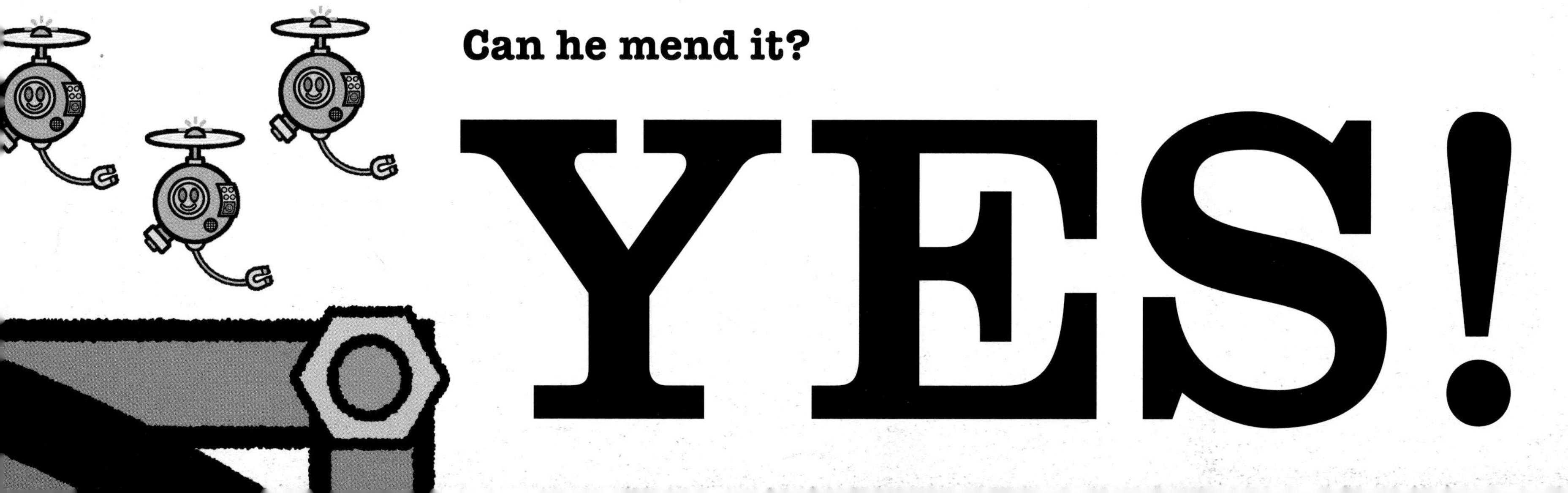

YES!

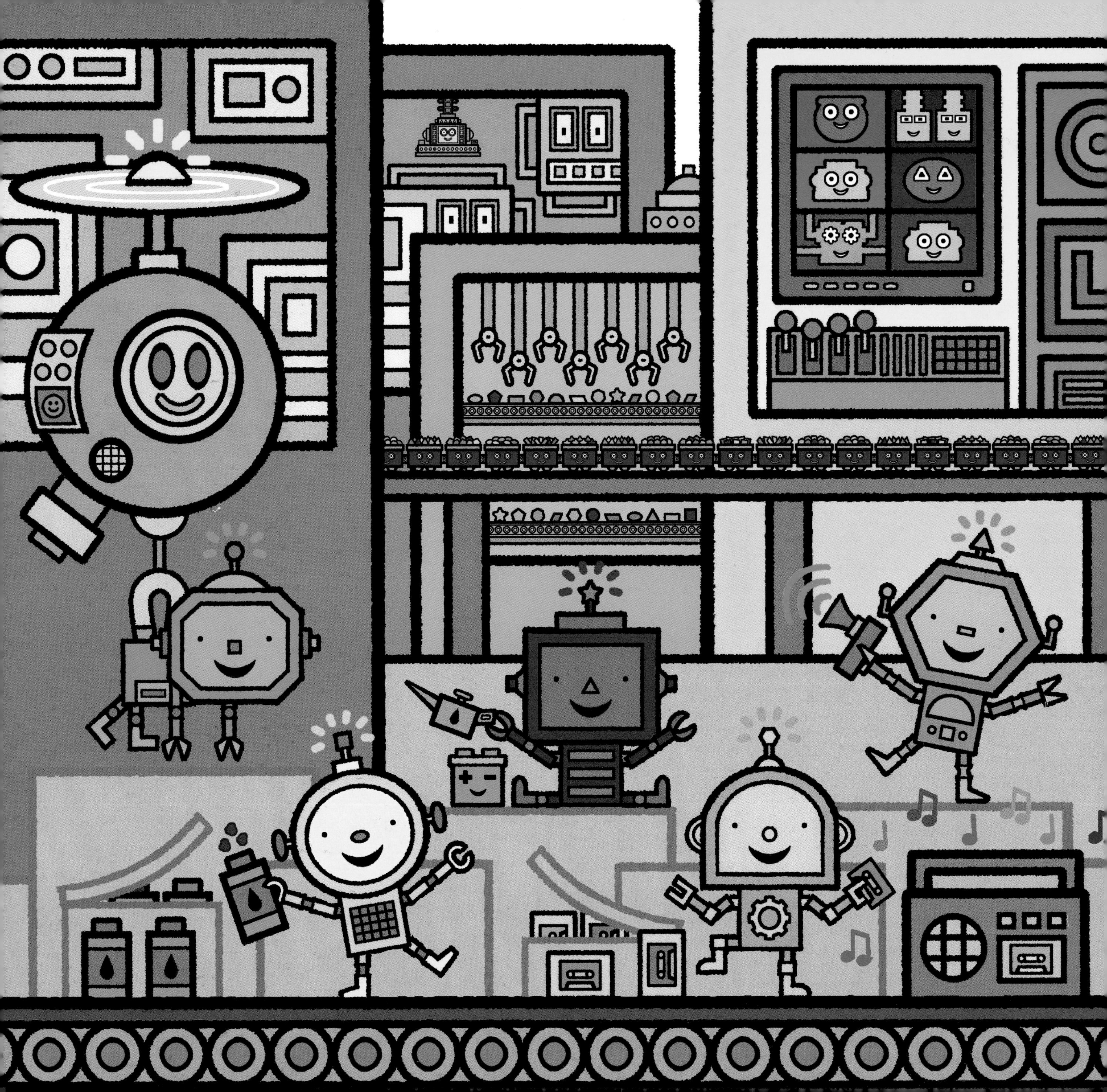

Hooray! The danger's over!

Their buzzers chirp and cheep!

Ten little robots all shout,

"BEEEEP!"

For Rex
M.B.

For E-BOT and I-BOT
S.R.

ORCHARD BOOKS

First published in Great Britain in 2018 by The Watts Publishing Group
This edition first published in 2018

1 3 5 7 9 10 8 6 4 2

A CIP catalogue record for this book is available from the British Library.

HB ISBN 978 1 40833 823 0
PB ISBN 978 1 40833 824 7

Printed and bound in China

Orchard Books
An imprint of Hachette Children's Group
Part of The Watts Publishing Group Limited
Carmelite House
50 Victoria Embankment
London EC4Y 0DZ

An Hachette UK Company
www.hachette.co.uk

www.hachettechildrens.co.uk